moths, rust

&

the things that stay

holly ducarte

Black Ladder Publishing
CANADA

Black Ladder Publishing

ISBN-13: 978-0-9958698-2-0

for all those who see light, hope, and the signature of truth all around them no matter how dark things get, and who know there is more beyond this world to look forward to

"Do not lay up for yourselves treasures on earth,
where moth and rust destroy and where thieves break in and steal, but lay up for yourselves treasures in Heaven, where neither moth nor rust destroys and where thieves do not break in and steal. For where your treasure is, there your heart will be also."

Matthew 6:19-21

Acknowledgments

God be praised for being with me during the peaks and valleys of life and gifting me the creativity to see and write things in a deep, and thoughtful way.

When this began as just a compilation of short poems on Wattpad with the simple title "rust", I didn't give it another thought to becoming anything more. But all the comments and compliments over the app, and the hard last two years we've all been through, made me consider it could grow into something special. So thank you Wattpadders for being a great boost! To my family, who are my cheerleaders that also offer constructive criticisms, which they know I thrive on...thank you always from the bottom of my heart.

To my "beta-reader moths" (Mandy, Nix, Jesse, Jordanna, Kelly, Andrea, and Suzanne), who offered me their feedback, cute hearts, and suggestions...I am so grateful. Many of you are writers and have families, and we all know time is precious. A special shoutout to Jordanna who went through every poem and gave notes and compliments. You absolutely went over and above.

To my "arc-reader moths" (Jesse, Josh, Stephen, Linda, Devin, Betsy, Carrie, and Brittany) who have been spreading the news online, leaving early reviews, and gave great ideas on tightening everything up. You all have offered continual support of my work, and give beautiful compliments. You took the nervous jitters out of me about this going out into the world. Thanks Josh for those DM pep talks and marketing strategies!

My little writing community online must always be thanked for lighting the fire under me to never give up. You all challenge me to meet goals, and improve overall as an author. On those dark days of wanting to give up, you've kept me at the keyboard.

Thanks also to the poetry fans I have, who also keep me motivated, and often direct message me that they aren't "poetry people" and yet really enjoy mine. How isn't that the best compliment a poet can ever hear?

And to you, dear reader, who decided to pick this book up, thank you. I hope it is timely, relatable, and finds a cherished spot on the library shelf of your heart.

holly ducarte

the fragility of the human experience

holly ducarte

FOE

sometimes i dip my heart in ice

yes, to test the depth of cold

how far can i handle the sting?

i think myself so bold – to persevere

yet i am afraid…

what if i never feel a thing?

what if even the sun hangs its shawl of warmth

around the chambers, and i still feel nothing?

numbness is a terrifying foe

masked with a friendly face, i know

- too well

SUNSET

i wanted to wander down the beaten track

ending up on the edge of the sunset

dancing as the brilliant sky faded to black

but i worried more about the road left behind

and being unable to find my way back

MAP OF SCARS

glorious morning

allow the shedding of yesterday

be it as ash gliding up from the fire

and dissipating into the readied dawn

for i will not be tethered to the past's burn

that dolorous fire

that reminds me where i singed

i am a map

and these scars are not my destiny

but the path to my destination

holly ducarte

ESCAPE

we longed for escape

the way morning dew drops away

from the heavy-headed flower

GROW

clip me away from the bunch

a swift snip like a flower in the garden

i do not wish to grow alongside the others

taken hostage by the night wind and its dithering sways

i want to rest in the sunlight of wisdom

and the truth that is shed in the days

IMAGINATION

after the rain

i'd watch the ripples in the glassy pond

and think of better tomorrows over bitter words

and being young - again

full of unspoiled imagination

DENIAL

the grass may grow

a distance from the sun

but it cannot deny

her far reaching arm

nor the warmth

of her embrace

LAUGHTER

when things whirl out of control

and the grim is on a trend

laughter has been, for me

a dear and loyal friend

QUIET

sometimes

the quiet of life

is deafeningly painful

MOST

often,

when we don't have much

we give the most

of what we've always needed

DRAMA

i lean on you, and leave behind

the cacophonous drama

broken pieces like shards of glass

that cut away harmony

and leave it to bleed

PLUMMET

what will become of the sparkling sky

when all the stars plummet

and there is nothing but dark

like a black hole in the heart

of the universe

TIRED

please don't tire of me

in all of life's fast paces

feasts upon silver platters

please don't tire of me

in fluid creations of your mind

and the idea that none of it matters

please don't tire of me

being filled with a sacred hope

for what better way to live this life?

what better way to cope?

SMILE

how mighty a smile can be

to showcase a thrill or a fancy

and yet, too, be a liar

SMALL

from time to time

we walk as tall as the trees

too proud to come down

but then life reminds us

how small we are

PAST

night is the most cathartic

when all the world around

is silent in a hum of sleep

my mind stays loud with the death of the past

memories of who i never wish to be again

CLEANSE

if you called me out on the water

i would go, though i cannot swim

i would let the salt sting my flesh

and cleanse my wickedness away

STUBBORN

to change is to acknowledge

there is so much more to learn

but you cannot see beyond your head

when unswervingly stubborn

GUILT

when patience dangles

on a thread

put your worries

quick to bed

for there is a far worse

sneaky foe

to contend with

after anger's blow

TURN AWAY

release the need of having to be perfect

you can't achieve this unreachable goal

but reflect and build character

and turn away from the things

that corrupt your soul

RECESSES

i have endured things

that tried to twist and blind

rifling through files of the past

in the recesses of my mind

but i tore up what was

and focused on what is

and there is nothing that compares

to this cognitive bliss

AUTHENTIC

to be honest is to fly

deception breaks wings

in the lie

FAKE

many are drawn

to the realism of humanity

and yet choose to live fake lives

SAFE

i was convinced being alone was safe

but it made me more susceptible

to the devil in the dark

S.O.S

they said they'd protect you

and yet you were surrounded

both land and sea

by wolves and sharks

BEAUTIFUL

why did i ever

let anyone persuade me

that appearance

is what makes us beautiful?

the healed heart is so much

the lovelier

MOTH

i may never be the butterfly

but i lifted my wings stronger

to get out of the dark

and you have no idea

what i have been through

as the moth

DROWNING

they called me weak

because i couldn't swim

but their hands were on my shoulders

forcing me down – forcing me in

MEMORIUM

the memories of her aged

but never faded

CANCELLED

you offend them when you have ideas

your face is dangerous with a mouth

how dare you make choices they themselves do not make

so your back must break – in the pressure it will take

to satisfy their ego

CREATIVITY

i fear the day

creativity is dried up

as paint upon an old brush

MASK

where did the smiling faces go

the jovial talks around town

when happening upon a friend

they are covered

and the eyes speak fear

and silence has created a distance

TELL

there were many times

i thought beautiful things

about those around me

why didn't i tell them?

when saying out loud

what i felt could have

brought life into their day

could have fixed a wound

STONE

there are evil eyes that no one sees

that remain ever watchful on us all

setting up traps to watch us fall

they see us as fleas

pests to do with whatever they please

but i am a person

with a heart that feels

not to be part of their money-making deals

they make us believe that we are alone

that our life is dictated by a cellular phone

i am not state property that you can own

i am made in the image of the Anointed One

the man we know to be God's only son

so as all creation continues to groan

those without sin, let them cast the first stone

holly ducarte

SCREEN

i couldn't embrace you behind a screen

or kiss your forehead while you wept

how important it is to have human touch

oh, how it heals and matters so much

SONG

there was a song around the city square

and people gathered to be heard

asking for peace and for the right to live

freedom was the word

but they came with batons and set up a gate

stifled the joyous song with their hate

prayers from all nations were lifted on high

that truth would win over the wickedest lie

HUMANITY

my heart has splinters

imbedded deep

it groans - for my wronged fellow man

i want to reach out in hope

and hold every hand

i whisper a strangled breath

this isn't…the…end

TRUTHFUL

they want to conceal

they want to condemn

but truth is not quashed

it hasn't an end

TIMES

wake up in those times

when they count on you

to stay sleeping

FORCE

how do they equate harmony with brutal force?

it must be too far to see within their ivory tower

or from off their trojan horse

SOLIDARITY

i dreamt the streets were ablaze

crowds fought around us

but you and i strode hand-in-hand

in the direction of solidarity

ISLANDS

lazing on the humid lawn

the clouds above looked like islands

they took my gaze away

from the chaotic stream of news

and the world on fire

GIVE

don't let them say

you are nothing more than a taker

a consumer of resources

when all your life

you've been known to give

FIRE

life may try to rake you

over simmering coals

but it forgets - you cannot be scathed

for you are a soul on fire

PURE

such mourning in the pureness of snow

tainted by the death of liberty

how much sadness it bears

with cracking tombs

amongst the glittering white

LAST

if there are things

that cannot last

let hope not be one of them

holly ducarte

tears and the beauty of the little things

holly ducarte

CAGE

i sewed the seams

severed my dreams

and i wore the cage

CASTLES

the clutches of naïve love

strangled the hope

of Pachelbel dreams

and castles by the sea

FOOLISH

i composed foolish songs

danced with stringed arms on display

you'd show the scissors

and then pull them away

PRIDE

there was nothing

in this world

that could separate us

...except your pride

SCARS

secrets you keep

claw at your heart

and leave

dangerous scars

CONTRAST

love feels like

taking the first breaths

goodbye feels like

a thousand deaths

MERGE

you merged with me

as wind enters the lungs

don't exhale me out

TALE-TELLER

there were days where inspiration floated

ceaselessly as dandelion seeds on the wind

there were so many reasons to pen poetry

so many reasons to write music

but time is different now…

i find i must grasp at anything that passes the breeze

where have all the seeds gone?

they left with you and your tale-teller heart

CLAIM

the eye is the arrow, finding its target

and - you kept moving

i just wanted you to slow down

so i could take my aim

but your heart was never mine to claim

STORY

if you come close

and reach out to touch me

will you take away from who i am

like tearing the corner off a book

or will you take up the pen

and add to my story?

CARDS

i built my walls

and set up the guards

but when you showed up

it all fell down like a house of cards

NOTHING

i was used to letting go

i began to speak in past tense

for nothing ever stayed…

until there was you

FIREFLY

you feel like the sweet olden days

of youth and joy

threads of hope like the tail of a kite

your warmth is welcome

like the cold dark overtaken by firefly light

TUNELESS

speak like a melody

and repair my

tuneless heart

ADAGIO

i adored you without knowing you

without meeting face to face

and, i wanted for you...grace

to see far more beyond time and space

because you spoke to my heart in some way

through the fabric of our makeup

a song would play...on shared strings

as a melody of blue

and vibrate eternity

with the deep adagio of you

WINDOW

i watched you through my window

like a damsel in a tower

how you flicked blades of grass

and skipped the rocks in my heart

you looked free and i felt stuck

you didn't need me - i needed you so much

your fascination with smiling

made me laugh to myself

this infatuation is likely no good for my health

i knew you would protect me

your moon eyes wax kind

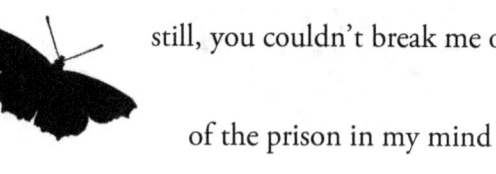

still, you couldn't break me out

of the prison in my mind

FRESH

you are fresh air

to this toxic life

AWAY

you understand my reluctance

to hold hands now

after the many times

those who should have held mine

pulled theirs away

RUBBER BAND

some people settle their hearts in the hands of others

you snapped yours inside my chest

a carefully projected rubber band flick

temporary painful sting

to have yours beating alongside mine

EXTRA

when the pieces

of my heart's puzzle were missing

you filled the caverns of emptiness

even when it meant blank places for you

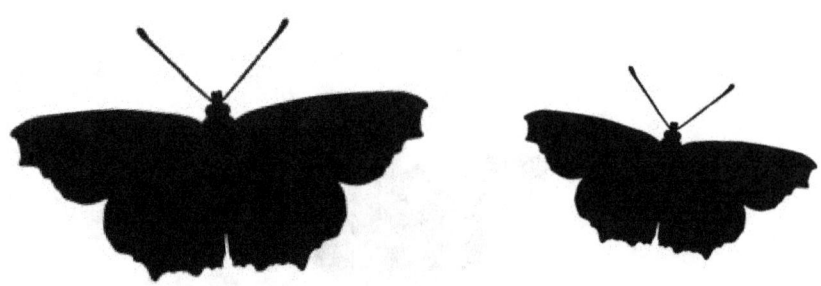

COLORS

i have thrown every part of myself

into the palette of your arms

now paint me into your life

brush your dreams with all my colors

SIMPLE LIFE

life could be simple

as fields of wild, white daisies

grazing against the weathered fence

and rusty, barbed wire

you and me in the shower

pretending to be trapped in April rain

water trails down our bare skin

our worn jeans in piles on the tile

soft music plays – distant

candlelight dances with shadows

let the walls whisper secrets about us

envious how our fresh love

contends with fire and all other elements

but we have no desire to boast

PRICELESS

you and i are strings of passion

carefully woven together

on the looms of desire

when we come together, we are a mosaic

a tapestry fit for the walls of royalty

and yet…priceless still

TRANSFORM

your lips are soft as Gabriel's wings

they drift over alabaster hips

and whisper ancient songs

intimate – as only Solomon knew

your heart was kept in higher places

ever restless with the world bargaining it

as if it were money changing hands

you entrust me with all that you are

together we burn with a desire

to hold one another's souls to the heat

and transform in refiner's fire

WANT

there is no finer tune

than your whisper in the night

the low rumble of your breath

like a thunderous cloud

your want for me is fierce

like storm winds unceasing

EBBING

the waves sparkled for you

whispered their affections in the ebbing

then carved the words

as a love note on the sands

BEGUILED

let me fashion a sonnet of love

about your mesmerising eyes

and watch me get beguiled

before i finish

STAGE

sway your melody in your artist's fingers

dance them upon my skin

i am your stage

move me more than Shakespeare

PLEASURES

let's go back to literature under ageless trees

and the romance of the wind

humming in time with the bees

to a moment of simple pleasures with linen and lace

i wish to imagine holding you in that place

BOOKS

just leave me with him

and all my books

so together we might escape

the world's harsh visage

LIBRARY

the passions which burn inside you

show in those determined eyes

makes me want to read you like a novel

drink you in like morning coffee

and wander the shelves of your library mind

BETWEEN

i can be found

in between the lines

of your most fond prose

WEATHER

the breeze strums

upon the strands of our hair

as we walk under heavy clouds

but we feel the heat of the sun

within our hearts

there is no gloom

that can dampen us now

nothing frightens anymore

our love is more powerful

and can weather any storm

MOVIE-TIME

beads of rain snaked down my window

and brooding skies made me think of fall

and you sliding into an auburn housecoat

smelling of dark wine and woodsmoke

how is it that on these nights

i long for the mystery of your silence

and the rasp of your calloused hands in mine

for a moment, we're in a movie

and someone's pressed the remote

pausing time

ROOT AND WIND

you find comfort in rooting

feet set on a firm foundation

whereas, i, the sinuous wind

strengthen your branches

while you grow and thrive

IMPERFECT

our love is memories and joy

imperfections and triumphs

stretchmarks and scars

this is what makes it exclusively ours

STRONG

it is a mystery how much he knows

how to firmly grip my heart

and yet keep it from

shattering into a hundred

thousand pieces

SHOWER

i whisper your name

while in the shower

for it refreshes as eucalyptus

and heals like balm to my weary bones

SPACE

cosmic eyes

those endless pathways

into pitch black

lined with silver and blue

a ring of Saturn

a vanishing star

a psalm of space

REALITY

i do not wish

to escape reality

with you in it

I AM THE CROW

you are the spontaneity of a day unplanned

i am the crow that feeds from the palm of your hand

the subtle light across your jaw, your nose

you're a museum's work of art in repose

you are the autumn gold cast upon the land

i am the crow that feeds from the palm of your hand

as the days shorten and the leaves sigh a prayer

i'll watch the wind dance and

 twirl in the strands of your hair

when i call to you, you won't understand

i am the crow that feeds from the palm of your hand

MOONLIGHT

i shall have no sleep in the beam

of the moon's plump opalescence

nor in the depth of his embrace

STRING

when we met

i tied a string

of remembrance around my heart

because i never wanted

to forget us

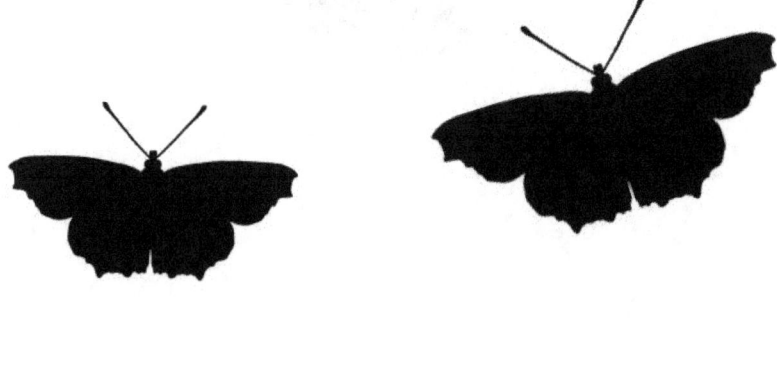

BREATHE

say nothing…shhh

rest and close your eyes

i just want to watch

your chest rise

KYANITE

i curled up in the crook of your arm

contented, as a cat lazing eagerly on a sunbeam

days were longer back then...

Father Time bore no name

all we knew consisted of cheap merlot

and jacuzzi water

we bathed one another to clean away our fears

how long could this bliss really last?

flicking impetuous wishes at low-lying stars...

we sang poetry to one another, tongue-tied

our bare skin became each other's satin sheet

your chest, my favourite pillow...

and still, i am unable to resist the rhythms

of your steady heart beat

the way you look down at me

with blue kyanite eyes

all the uncertainty of the past

washing away on their shores

BILLION

a billion words shared between us

and yet my heart remains stunned

into utter silence

when you're next to me

ROMANCE

i would rather clothes on the floor

and a love-messed bed

then a perfect room

and a romance dead

BIRDHEART

you've always known me to have a bird-heart

and you wouldn't dare cage it

you hold it well, as it's restless

there were times it flew away

but it always came back

it knows you best

home is where this bird-heart rests

PARENTS

we've been on so many adventures together

but none compare to

the day you and i became parents

and lifted our little one up

from out of the womb

into a brave new world

FRIEND AND FAMILY

you were every wish i ever spoke in my youth

every plan i ever made in my heart

i know it now more than ever, until eternity

you are my friend and my family

my place of solace in an unpeaceful world

a touch of heaven upon cursed ground

fashioned for me in all the day to day

a strong shoulder in the come what may

i am blessed in every wow and mundane

you are my extravagant and you are my plain

the beauty for ashes beyond the pain

because…

you were every wish i ever spoke in my youth

every plan i ever made in my heart

i know it now more than ever, until eternity

you are my friend and my family

MAN OF HONOR

your hands are the sword

that pierced and entered my heart

a heart once of stone

and impenetrable steel

your eyes hold the nobility of kings

the strands of your hair are made of gold and fire

your heart is spirited and strong

your body is a shield of loyalty

you stand proud, but have the humility of Earth

what a man of honor you are

one to be crowned, yet wears none

nor seeks renown or fortune

but burns with a desirous flame

one that devours my love

and swallows whole my loneliness

in this life – when the tides ever turn

i will fight by your side

i will be your queen

and our kingdom will prevail

whenever i am wrapped in your arms

JOURNEY

as the clock of time ticks round and round

and life shows as creases on our faces

you will always be my partner

on the journey toward heaven

CELESTIAL

when words fail to escape my mouth

they must be told through my hands

such delicate hands know how to move

with intricate words

upon paper, i write my dream

the one reoccurring

where we ask God to speak out new stars

the way he did in the beginning

as he obliges, we slip through space

as bright as celestial bodies

our hearts are weightless and free

holly ducarte

treasures of heaven

holly ducarte

NEW LIFE

come up from the river

walk out from the tomb

you are no longer the old

you've become someone new

BUOY HANDS

the tide has shifted, and i look out at the storm

contrast to your buoy hands that keep me afloat

i've wondered at how easy i might drown

if i didn't have you

STORM

the boat in our mind's sea

might break in the storms of heartache

but we can find safe haven

on salvation's shores

GATE

hurry quick

before it's too late

there is only one way

through the narrow gate

PILLOW

it can be said

that we find rest

on the soft prayers placed

upon the pillows

of our beds

TRUE JUDGE

you have loved me

through my asymmetries

of bone, of scar, of heart

i am not asked to stand upon

an invisible scale that judges

where scrutinizing eyes

believe they know who i am

and wish to see me brought low

even with the gavel, you do not use it

aware that beauty still exists in my flaws

with your hands, you have knit

my brokenness and pled my case

my transgressions washed in blood not my own

i can never thank you enough for this

even unto eternity

CERTAIN

i have not seen you, and yet i believe

you said a blessing over me

for i did not doubt your marked hands

or the piercings of your feet

i am certain of your return

and the coming day we will meet

DOORS

there are many chamber doors

in a heart, soul, and mind

but only you have been able to

unlock them all

and walk within mine

THE ONE

how can i stay the same

after meeting the one who purifies hearts?

how can i cling to death

when he shows me life everlasting?

how can i turn my back

when his got torn in my place?

how can i long to be bound

when he broke sin's chains around me?

i will not pretend i do not know

the one who saves

FOUNDATION

as fragile as the dust

of butterflies

as strong as the

foundations of heaven

SPIRIT

if you chip away at my exterior

you will not find just flesh and bone

but also spirit

and the beginnings of a place

not of this world

EVEN

even in my most frail moments

i have known your strength

even in my most mournful times

i have known your joy

even in my blunders through shadow

i have not lost sight of you

COMPANY

to open your word

is to taste knowledge

to savour history

and linger in the honor

of your company

LIGHT

a shadow came to steal my light

but couldn't find it

because it lived in you

HEART OF THE FOREST

there is a tree

beating like a drum

and the roots are deep

immovable

on the branches

are many colored leaves

some grafted amongst the lot

fruit grows

offered to those

who are empty

but they refuse

eating only from the

iron trees of industry

teeth bleeding

breaking in the tasting

their soul rusts, malnourished

they blame the living tree

and try to break its limbs in angst

still, it stands strong and majestic

drum, drum, drumming

for they can never remove

the heart of the forest

DRY BONES

it is a call to hearts

to awake from the grave

put flesh to dry bones

to embolden the brave

no more self-exaltation

put away the moths and the rust

clean your newfound skin from sin

cast off all the dying dust

PHYSICIAN

resuscitator of tainted flesh

and deadened hearts – turned black by decay

and sin's sharp edges

you are the great physician

SUPERNATURAL

i have seen you in the whimsy of the natural

but i have felt you in the winds

of the supernatural

the lesser known place in the spirit

that can never be broken

HOLD

hold the hands that were pierced for you

hold the heart that was speared

hold the body marred by their hate

hold the face that they jeered

hold the feet that tread upon snakes

hold the head full of thorns

hold the hair that is stained with tears

hold the mouth as it mourns

hold the man who takes away sin

hold the Maker of new things

hold the Prince of peacefulness

behold the King of kings

WAVES

we are a wave

and in that moment

when we touch shore

for the final time

let us say we touched love

let us leave behind pebbles of calm

and in our receding, reflecting light

from the one who gave us life

and is himself light

let this wave have spoken

volumes of the mighty ocean

that is our God

REVERENCE

from the dirt we began

and thus, are nurtured by nature

lulled into reverence of our Creator

while gazing upon the beauty

SINNER

i have tripped over my feet

in this life more than i care to count

and i've worn shame

and the heavy cloak of darkness

until i tripped again

touched your garment

and was healed of my ailing soul

WASH

i crawled - bedraggled and thirsty

and you gave me living water

you picked me up and washed my filth away

i am new and want for nothing

RED

the cross

is my bed

where i rest

my weary head

and because you ran

with red

i have eternal life

instead

PERFECT

this world calls for perfection

but then fails to reach its own height

it forgets that truth is not found in the shadows

it is found in the light

holly ducarte

RESTORE

there came a whisper in the burning forest

that climbed up the treetops

reaching limbs toward the skies

restore us, restore us

an answer echoed, "soon."

WEARY

when i am shaken by the evil of mankind

and my heart grieves for your embrace

i cling to the knowledge that one day

the tears will be wiped from my wearied face

YOU ARE

in a world of deserts

you are living water

that never stops its flow

in a world of darkness

you are a burning light

that never stunts its glow

you are the wisdom in the silence

the ever open door

in a people that worship riches

you are the one who brings them low

in a people who are blinded

you are the one who makes them see

i know this all because

you are the life that lives in me

WARRIOR

you are the red cord on our door

the hedge of protection in the wild

the armour and strength

that make us warriors

PRAISES

all i saw was the top

of the hole i had dug

your fingernails tasted mud

white robe stained in blood

you stepped into the mire of my life

never made me feel the shame

your face was soft and void of blame

you called me by a newfound name

pulling me out of my pit of despair

i shouted praises from the land to the sea

you came from heaven to set me free

your grace is sufficient for me

FORMLESS

do not let them scoff at you

set themselves up on high

break their pillars and idols

dash their pride against the rock

without you, they are formless – unmade

unwise and steeped in lies

HOLY SPIRIT

the fiery arrows soar

but we do not scatter

we take up the shield and stand

the enemy is defenceless

against the spirit's hand

CROSS

let my hands grow strong

from clutching so tightly

to that old rugged cross

GIFTS

every good thing in my life came from you

in the bounty of your endless heart

and the breadth of your being

BLESSED

there is a blessed land in all of us

that cannot be conquered

VENTURE

i called myself an adventurer

went without tools or skill – and no will

got tangled in the weeds of temptation's thrill

until you cut down my binds with the sword

REDIRECTION

so many paths i fumbled down

wide and yet full of traps

none ever led me to you

i went back and wandered

all through the night

took the narrow road

toward those slivers of light

i would chance it all

it would take much of my courage

to breathe truth and speak it

an integrity and conviction

every ounce of my might

to stand in your grace

and be given my sight

for that moment of mercy

bending a knee to surrender

giving away my stony heart

so my soul could remember

had always known what was right

hands reach up to your face

i relinquish the fight

ALKALINE

you can't dabble in the secret evils

of the world and call it alkaline

it leaves acid trails and chemical burns

that carve out your soul and your mind

CLAY

who are we to blame the potter

for our choices and shame

clay has no place to defame

the Maker's holy name

holly ducarte

THIRST

you deserved much better than sour wine

and cracked lips, yearning – pursed

you breathlessly worded, "i thirst"

my sin put you on that tree

now all i long to ever do

is thirst for the righteousness of you

GETHSEMANE

when doubt tries to filter in

i think of how my Lord knelt in the garden

of the verdant Gethsemane

bowed his head and prayed for me

holly ducarte

STAND

arise dear saints

you are not beat down

keep yourselves from being shaken

you are in victory

do not be silent

shout that you aren't forsaken

you have a purpose

were made to stand tall

your future cannot be taken

AUTOMATON

i will not stand by

and watch them

grind metal into your back

turn all the soft

into hard, feelingless frame

replace mind with gear

flush out artery

with electricity and wire

your blood is alive

it shouts out for relief

deny the thief!

deny the thief!

REFLECTION

when you take me near still water

i want to look inside the pool

and see you inside my reflection

GOOD NEWS

continue to lift me up

oh, Lord of heaven

remind me of the grandeur

of the good news

when i act like i've forgotten

TEMPTATION

go away temptation

leave me be

i do not want your lies

and your blasphemy

i do not want fame

or fleeting desire

i do not wish to owe a debt

that your sin will require

sing your siren song

i will stopper my ears

you cannot have my soul

or eternity's years

you have nothing that lasts

or holds truth or merit

you are nothing more

than the devil's parrot

go away temptation

leave me be

you have no power or control

over the spirit inside me

LION

guide my life to valour

for i am a timid lamb

let me feel the lion's roar

build up in my throat

CORINTHIANS

the days may not always be kind

or extend a helping hand

but one moment is not the full story

you can keep pressing on

though the present feels heavy

for that eternal weight of glory

GOSPEL

if the eyes of heaven can smile

upon the shoulders of Saul

and lift the burden of sin that sat there

and retitle him Paul

you needn't be afraid to come to the altar

and seek forgiveness and cleansing, too

for the gospel is about Jesus' finished work

not about what you've done or can do

RISEN

i sing as the birds sing

praising the name of the King

the Master and Lord of everything

all the marvels he has made

my penalty he has paid

paradise power displayed

as he rose and defeated the grave

REVELATION

upon wings

i set my dreams

and i hear a thrum

of a distant drum

"woe! woe!" - it calls

break all the walls

knees shall bow

the time is now

moths, rust & the things that stay

holly ducarte

WHAT DID YOU THINK OF THIS POETRY COLLECTION?

Please consider leaving a thoughtful review for Holly on your preferred book review/retailer site. Other ideas on how to support this collection? Word of mouth, suggesting it in your libraries and bookstores, promoting it on your social media pages, gifting a copy, and using the book in giveaways.

Thank you!

THE GOSPEL OF JESUS

"For God so loved the world that He gave his one and only Son, that whosoever believes in Him, shall not perish but have everlasting life."—John 3:16

"He himself bore our sins in His body on the tree, that we might die to sin and live to righteousness. By His wounds you have been healed."—1 Peter 2:24

"For the wages of sin is death, but the free gift of God is eternal life in Christ Jesus our Lord."—Romans 6:23

Because of the fall and our sinful nature, we are separated from our Creator and stand condemned in our depravity. There is nothing we can do on our own to make ourselves right to stand before Him, for He is a Holy God. But, as a result of His great love for humankind, He gifted us Jesus Christ, who willingly left the throne of heaven to be our Messiah. Jesus lived the perfect life we could not, and He taught truth and the way of salvation. He said:

"I am the way, the truth, and the life. No one comes to the Father except through me."—John14:6

However, God's Son was rejected and put to death by crucifixion. Knowing this would happen beforehand, Jesus also made it clear about His life:

"No man takes it from me, but I lay it down of myself. I have power to lay it down, and I have power to take it again. This commandment have I received of my Father."—John 10:18

Our deliverance was accomplished through Him. He said, "It is finished," taking the weight and judgment of our sin upon Himself. On the third day, Jesus rose from the grave, overcoming sin and death. If we believe Jesus is our Savior who atoned for us, we are free from condemnation. We now wear His spotless robe of righteousness upon us.

"Therefore there is now no condemnation for those in Christ Jesus who walk not after the flesh, but after the Spirit."—Roman 8:1

God asks us to turn away from our wrong doings and fleshly desires that end up costing us and, oftentimes, others. Bad choices, whether they feel good or not, have penalties, and they distract our lives away from seeing things through the lens of the Holy Spirit. We become as slaves to our selfish desires. But we are set free and no longer a slave when we have faith in Jesus Christ as the full payment of our sins. We can live in a way that honors His sacrifice so that others may see the light of Christ in us.

So, be renewed by the Lord Jesus. Believe in what He's done for you. For you matter and are treasured. God bless you.

"You are the light of the world. A town built on a hill cannot be hidden. Neither do people light a lamp and put it under a bowl. Instead they put it on its stand, and it gives light to everyone in the house."—Matthew 5:14-15

holly ducarte

ABOUT THE AUTHOR

Holly Ducarte is a Canadian creative fiction author and an award-winning poet. Her other written works are Confetti Confessions, The Light Over Broken Tide, and Black Worm which is a short story that was nominated for a literary award in 2020 and published in an anthology titled Just Words vol 4. She also writes on Wattpad. Holly lives a cozy and simple life in a modest lake town with her husband, daughter, and two cats. She enjoys connecting with readers and other authors on Instagram, growing in the Christian faith, taking photographs while on nature walks, reading, gardening, antique shopping, listening to indie and big-band music, singing, shameless dancing, and good food with tea and coffee.

Find out more and follow her newsletter at:
www.hollyducarte.com

holly ducarte

moths, rust & the things that stay